—— The First ——

ROMAN
MYSTERIES
QUIZ BOOK

THE ROMAN MYSTERIES

by Caroline Lawrence

Look out for . . .
The Code of Romulus
The Second Roman Mysteries Quiz Book
Trimalchio's Feast and Other Mini-mysteries

THE FIRST ROMAN MYSTERIES QUIZ BOOK

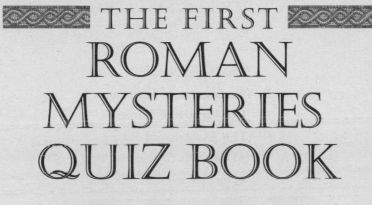

Caroline Lawrence

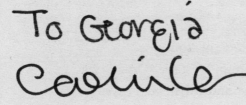

To Georgia

Caroline

Orion
Children's Books

First published in Great Britain in 2007
by Orion Children's Books
a division of the Orion Publishing Group Ltd
Orion House
5 Upper St Martin's Lane
London WC2H 9EA

3 5 7 9 10 8 6 4

The Orion Publishing Group's policy is to use papers that are natural,
renewable and recyclable products and made from wood grown in
sustainable forests. The logging and manufacturing processes are expected
to conform to the environmental regulations of the country of origin.

A catalogue record for this book is available from the British Library

ISBN-13 978 1 84255 594 1

Printed in Great Britain by Clays Ltd, St Ives plc

www.orionbooks.co.uk

CONTENTS

WELCOME!

I write mysteries set in ancient Roman times. In my books, I have created four children who are detectives. As a writer of historical fiction, I am a detective, too. Artefacts are my clues and the primary sources are my witnesses. They help me solve the mystery of 'What It Was Like To Live In Roman Times'.

Artefacts are the things that people used in past times. In Latin, the word artefact means 'something made by hand'. Artefacts reveal the sight and feel and smell and sound of the ancient world. The Pompeian fresco of a forlorn little boy, for example, shows what one Roman child looked like. A clay oil-lamp from Roman Egypt gives a spooky light from its smoky flame. The silky smooth beeswax on a replica wax tablet smells like honey, and if you push too hard with the bronze stylus you can hear the wood crunch underneath. A sponge-stick would have smelled like vinegar and poo, because when it wasn't being used as ancient toilet paper, it was probably sitting in a beaker of vinegar.

The people who lived in Roman times died long ago, but they can still bear witness to what it was like back then. They testify through the primary sources, the things written in ancient times. From tombstones we learned that parents grieved the death of a two-year-old just as much as we do today, even though in those days many children died before the age of three. From poetry we learn that young men burned with passionate love, just as men and women still do today. From shopping lists we learn that Romans got cold feet sometimes and wore socks under their sandals. From their philosophical writings we know the ancient Romans wondered about the meaning and purpose of life, just as we still do. Romans could be pompous, funny, sarcastic, sincere, boring, exciting, superstitious and sceptical. Just like us.

They chewed gum, used toothpicks, dyed their hair and had indoor plumbing. Just like us. They crucified runaway slaves, gave their twelve-year-old daughters to be married and watched men kill each other for amusement. Not so much like us.

This is the puzzle that fascinates me the most. As I read the primary sources, play with the artefacts and write my books, this is the *real* mystery I am trying to solve: how were the Romans like us, and how were they not like us?

I would like to thank the other contributors, young and old(er), who have helped compile the questions for this book. We all had fun thinking up the questions and we hope you have as much fun answering them. I would especially like to thank my editor Jon, who let me use some of my favourite artefacts and primary sources.

Vale! (farewell) Caroline

MAP QUIZZES

In every Roman Mystery there are maps at the front to show you where the story's action takes place. Can you match the place name to the letter that appears beside it on the map?

OSTIA IN AD79

1. Roman Gate   *Answer:* ....
2. Marina Gate   *Answer:* ....
3. Flavia's house   *Answer:* ....
4. Temple of Hercules   *Answer:* ....
5. Laurentum Gate   *Answer:* ....
6. Forum of the Corporations   *Answer:* ....
7. Theatre   *Answer:* ....
8. Avita's Grave   *Answer:* ....
9. Temple of Rome and
   Augustus   *Answer:* ....
10. Synagogue   *Answer:* ....

For the answers to these questions, turn to page 101.

the lighthouse and
the new harbour

RIVER TIBER

Grain
and
Grape

River
Harbour

baths

ware-
houses

warehouses

granaries

ware-
houses

warehouses

baths

mills

bakeries

baths

warehouses

baths

F

dunes

shrine of the
crossroads

temple of Jupiter,
Juno & Minerva

apartments

fish
market

baths

Decumanus   Maximus

fountain

the
hydra
fountain

A

Marina Street

Marina
harbour

North

West

East

South

Marina baths

dunes

warehouses

K

beach

10

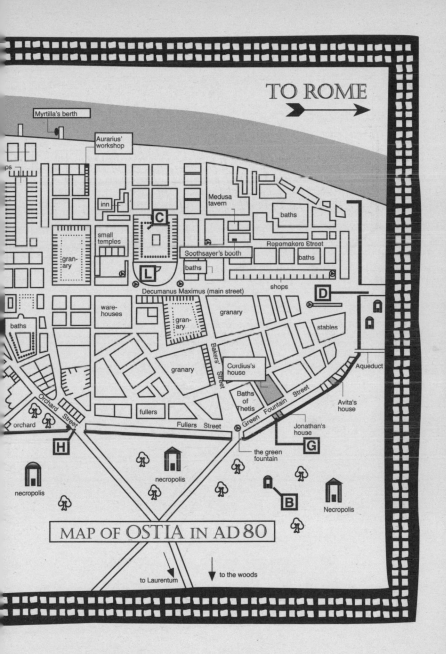

TO ROME

Myrtilla's berth

Aurarius' workshop

ps

inn

Medusa tavern

baths

small temples

C

Ropomakoro Street

granary

Soothsayer's booth

baths

baths

L

Decumanus Maximus (main street)

shops

D

warehouses

granary

granary

granary

stables

baths

granary

Bakers' Street

Curdius's house

Aqueduct

fullers

Baths of Thetis

Avita's house

Orchard Street

Fullers Street

Green Fountain Street

Jonathan's house

orchard

H

the green fountain

G

B

necropolis

necropolis

Necropolis

necropolis

MAP OF OSTIA IN AD 80

to Laurentum

to the woods

II

GAIUS'S FARM

11. Impluvium   *Answer:* ....
12. Latrine   *Answer:* ....
13. Stables   *Answer:* ....
14. Slaves' quarters   *Answer:* ....
15. Library   *Answer:* ....
16. Portico   *Answer:* ....
17. Atrium   *Answer:* ....
18. Toolshed   *Answer:* ....
19. Wine cellar   *Answer:* ....
20. Well   *Answer:* ....

For the answers to these questions, turn to page 101.

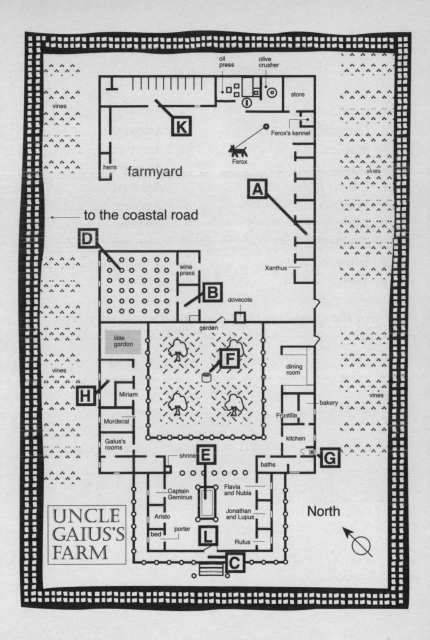

oil press

olive crusher

store

vines

K

Ferox's kennel

hens

farmyard

Ferox

to the coastal road

A

D

wine press

B

Xanthus

dovecote

garden

little garden

F

dining room

vines

H

Miriam

vines

Mordecai

bakery

Frustilla

Gaius's rooms

kitchen

shrine

E

baths

G

Captain Geminus

Flavia and Nubia

North

Aristo

Jonathan and Lupus

bed

porter

L

UNCLE
GAIUS'S
FARM

Rufus

C

13

21. Appian Way   *Answer:* ....
22. Pyramid of Cestius   *Answer:* ....
23. Flaminian Way   *Answer:* ....
24. Golden House   *Answer:* ....
25. Circus Maximus   *Answer:* ....
26. Capitoline Hill   *Answer:* ....
27. River Tiber   *Answer:* ....
28. Roman Forum   *Answer:* ....
29. Imperial Palace   *Answer:* ....
30. Colossus   *Answer:* ....

For the answers to these questions, turn to page 102.

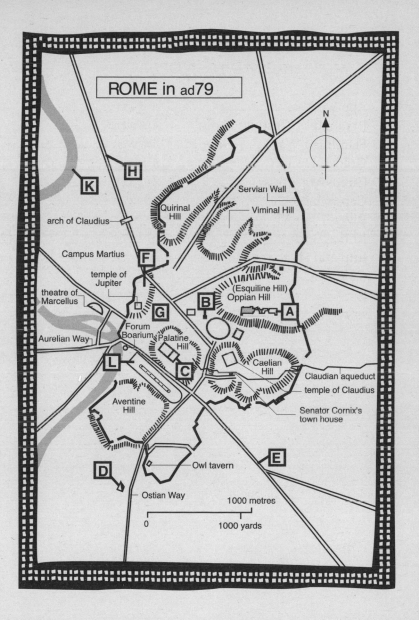

ROME in ad79

N

Servian Wall

Quirinal Hill

Viminal Hill

arch of Claudius

Campus Martius

temple of Jupiter

theatre of Marcellus

(Esquiline Hill) Oppian Hill

Forum Boarium

Palatine Hill

Aurelian Way

Caelian Hill

Claudian aqueduct

temple of Claudius

Senator Cornix's town house

Aventine Hill

Owl tavern

Ostian Way

1000 metres

0   1000 yards

H

K

F

G

B

A

L

C

D

E

THE THIEVES
OF OSTIA

Hercules completes his twelfth labour
by bringing the three-headed hellhound
Cerberus to King Eurystheus.

(Illustration based on a vase from around 530 BC)

31. In *The Thieves of Ostia* on what date does Flavia Gemina solve her first mystery?

32. Captain Geminus needs his amethyst signet ring to seal letters and documents, but it also has sentimental value for him. Why?

33. What are the names of the mythological twins known as the Gemini?

34. What is Captain Geminus's pet name for his daughter?

35. What is the necropolis?

36. What is the main street of Ostia called?

37. Name three horrible physical features of Venalicius, the slave-dealer?

38. The Emperor Nero began to persecute Christians during his reign. According to Jonathan, what crime did Nero accuse them of?

39. How much money does Flavia receive in exchange for the treasures found in the magpie's nest?

40. Why shouldn't Flavia have asked Nubia to recline?

41. At Flavia's dinner party everyone tells of the most revolting food they have ever been offered. Can you match the food with the person?

1. Flavia	A. Whole charred quail
2. Jonathan	B. Sheep's eyeball
3. Captain Geminus	C. Chalk and sand in bread
4. Mordecai	D. Human finger
5. Miriam	E. Rotten fishhead

42. Who is Titus Cordius Atticus?

43. Flavia's mother died in childbirth, the most common cause of death in adult women during Roman times. How old was Flavia when her mother died?

44. What is the name of Jonathan's watchdog?

45. According to some scholars, most well-to-do Roman families had an average of four slaves. When Flavia first meets Jonathan, how many slaves does his family have?

46. When a girl dies of rabies as a result of a dogbite, Doctor Mordecai gives this affliction a Greek name, which means 'fear of water'. What does he call rabies?

47. What do Flavia and her friend mistake Lupus for when they first see him?

48. What is the Dog Throw?

49. When Flavia and Lupus investigate Avita's house, they find an encaustic portrait of her. What is an encaustic painting made of?

50. Why do the detectives go to visit the harbourmaster, Lucius Cartilius Poplicola?

51. Where does Jonathan try to take his friends to hide and escape from the slave-dealers?

52. How does Pliny advise staving off an attack by ferocious dogs?

53. Ostia, the port of Rome, had a lighthouse modelled on the famous lighthouse of Alexandria. Who dies by jumping from Ostia's lighthouse?

54. What is unique about the way that rabid dogs run?

55. What does Lupus find in the store-room which gives Flavia a vital clue to solving the crime?

56. What animal appears on the seal of Captain Geminus's patron?

57. Flavia dreams of the three-headed hound who guards the gates of the Underworld. What is the name of this mythical creature?

58. What substance allows the detectives to be certain of the villain's identity?

59. Rome's ninth emperor dies at the end of June AD 79. What is his name?

60. According to Pliny's *Natural History*, the fiercest watchdog is a hybrid from India. It has a dog for a mother. Which animal is its father?

For the answers to these questions, turn to page 102.

CLOTHES AND FASHION

Featuring Questions by
Guest Quizmaster Emma Yeomans

61. In *The Thieves of Ostia*, what is the man sobbing beside the tomb wearing and who is he?

62. Can you match the image on the ring to its owner:
    1. A dolphin   A. Rectina
    2. A coiling snake   B. Susannah bat Jonah
    3. Castor and Pollux   C. Thalia
    4. A wolf   D. Emperor Titus
    5. Two clasped hands   E. Captain Geminus
    6. A boar   F. Lupus
    7. A dove   G. Cordius

63. What does Lupus's tunic smell of when he wakes up at Jonathan's house for the first time in *The Thieves of Ostia*?

64. In *The Secrets of Vesuvius,* what is Miriam wearing when she collects ivy and honeysuckle at Uncle Gaius's farm?
    A) A lavender tunic
    B) A lavender stola
    C) A lavender toga

65. Can you match the names of these gems and semi-precious stones to their colour:

1. Amethyst	A. Green
2. Aquamarine	B. Sea-blue
3. Sardonyx	C. Blue
4. Tiger's-eye	D. Lavender
5. Sapphire	E. Black
6. Lapis lazuli	F. Dark blue
7. Emerald	G. Golden brown
8. Jet	H. Apricot

66. What do Clio's younger sisters tie to Scuto's fur in *The Secrets of Vesuvius*?

67. Which of the children wear fashionable sea-green tunics to a dinner party at the Villa Limona in *The Pirates of Pompeii*?

68. In *The Pirates of Pompeii*, what does the Roman emperor wear?
A) Purple toga
B) Purple palla
C) Purple tunic

69. In *The Assassins of Rome*, why does Aristo describe his toga as 'insufferably hot'?

70. When the four detectives meet Phrixus again (in *The Assassins of Rome*) he is wearing a freedman's hat. What shape is it?
A) Flat like a cap

B) Cone-shaped
C) Cylindrical

71. In *The Dolphins of Laurentum*, Pliny gives Miriam gold earrings in the shape of which creature?

72. The detectives meet Vibia in *The Twelve Tasks of Flavia Gemina*. What kind of wool is Vibia's distinctive cloak made from?
    A) Wool from a goat's stomach
    B) Wool from a camel's stomach
    C) Wool from a sheep's stomach

73. What does Miriam wear to her wedding at the end of *The Twelve Tasks of Flavia Gemina*?
    A) Saffron-yellow robe, orange cloak, white veil
    B) White robe, saffron-yellow cloak, bright orange veil
    C) White robe, saffron-yellow cloak, black veil

74. In *The Twelve Tasks of Flavia Gemina*, Cartilia wears earrings shaped like which hero's weapon?

75. Can you match the following items of clothing to their definitions?
    1. Stola   A. Amulet made of metal or leather worn by freeborn children
    2. Bulla   B. Dress mainly worn by married women
    3. Palla   C. Cloak worn by women over the head or round the waist

76. What is distinctive about the tunic of a workman like a blacksmith?

77. Can you match the colour of cloth with its association?
    1. Black   A. Extravagant
    2. Leek-green   B. Mourning
    3. Brown   C. Effeminate
    4. Purple   D. Humble
    5. Saffron-yellow   E. Political candidate
    6. Unbleached (beige)   F. Imperial
    7. Brilliant white   G. Marriage
    8. Scarlet   H. Poor

78. What garment usually worn by male citizens is also worn by women of ill-repute?

79. Which one of the following garments is not known to Romans?
    1. Underwear
    2. Clogs
    3. Waterproof hooded cloaks
    4. Socks
    5. Platform shoes
    6. Ties
    7. Metal-studded boots

80. Which one of the following accessories was not known to Romans?
    1. Parasols
    2. Umbrella hats
    3. Broad-brimmed travelling hats

4. Sundial wristwatches
5. Nose-rings
6. Thumb-rings
7. Facial beauty patches

For the answers to these questions, turn to page 103.

WRITERS AND WRITING

81. According to Mordecai, what is the name of the Jews' holy scriptures?

82. How many scrolls (i.e. books) are in the *Aeneid*?

83. What is distinctive about Admiral Pliny's handwriting?

84. What was Admiral Pliny's first book?

85. Which famous natural history comprises thirty-seven volumes?

86. What is the name of the tool used for writing on wax tablets?

87. Which one of the following materials did Romans *not* write on?
    1. Ivory
    2. Paper
    3. Thin strips of wood
    4. Wax tablets
    5. Papyrus
    6. Parchment
    7. Cloth

88. Who wrote *The Georgics*?

89. Pliny wrote about a dolphin who let men ride on it. The governor wanted to honour this creature. What substance did he use for this purpose – and what was its effect on the dolphin?

90. Who runs the bookstall in Ostia's Forum?

91. When Flavia visits Vibia she sees a scroll with a play about Hercules. Which Greek playwright wrote this play?

92. Flavia also finds a scroll of Greek myths in Vibia's house. Which Greek author wrote them?

93. Miriam names her pet sparrow after a famous Latin poet who wrote about his girlfriend's dead sparrow. Name the poet.

94. Which book of the Hebrew scriptures is Mordecai quoting in his love letter to Susannah, where he writes, 'With one glance of your eyes you have captured my heart'?

95. Which poet wrote about the villa of Pollius Felix?

96. In *The Thieves of Ostia* Mordecai says, 'If the owner of the house had known at what time the thief was coming, he would have kept watch and not let his house be broken into.' Who is he quoting?

97. In *The Secrets of Vesuvius*, Phrixus is Admiral Pliny's scribe. What special piece of writing equipment does he have?

98. When the friends first meet Lupus in *The Thieves of Ostia*, he cannot write. However, he is a quick learner and in *The Secrets of Vesuvius* he writes his first word on a wax tablet. What is it?

99. In *The Secrets of Vesuvius*, Admiral Pliny says he prefers to eat at a table rather than reclining. Why?

100. One of the few Latin words beginning with 'K' means the first day of the month. What is it?

For the answers to these questions, turn to page 104

THE SECRETS
OF VESUVIUS

The blacksmith god Vulcan returns to
Mount Olympus, riding a donkey.
*(Illustration based on a Greek red-figure
vase of around 425 BC)*

101. Nine years before *The Secrets of Vesuvius* takes place, Jonathan's father took him and his sister out of Jerusalem. Why?

102. What is the name of the sea monster who attacks Jonathan at the start of the story?

103. Captain Geminus doesn't think Ostia is a safe place for children in the summer. Where has he decided to send them instead?

104. Why is Flavia alarmed to see a black-and-yellow-striped sail?

105. Admiral Pliny is rescued from a boat which capsized because of what creature?

106. The young detectives each receive gifts for rescuing Admiral Pliny. Can you match the object to its recipient?
    1. Flavia   A. Tiger's-eye earrings
    2. Jonathan   B. A signet ring
    3. Nubia   C. A herb pouch
    4. Lupus   D. A scroll.

107. According to the blacksmith, where will the solution to the graffiti riddle lead?

108. Why are the streets of Pompeii always wet?

109. Who is the elder of the two Geminus brothers?

110. Why are some Greek pots called 'red-figure'?

111. What is a satyr?

112. In Roman imagery, how would you recognise Vulcan?

113. Why did Uncle Gaius never marry?

114. The eruption which destroyed Pompeii was the first recorded eruption of Vesuvius. According to scholars, on what date did this occur?

115. What time do the shops close and the baths open in Pompeii and other Roman towns?

116. What surveillance device do the four young detectives build, so they can watch the road from Pompeii to Stabia?

117. Clio is the girl Flavia and her friends meet at the villa on the deserted road. She has eight sisters. What two things do all the sisters have in common?

118. Which of the following is *not* one of the nine muses?
    1. Clio
    2. Thalia
    3. Melpomene

4. Calliope
5. Euterpe
6. Historia
7. Terpsichore
8. Erato
9. Polyhymnia
10. Urania

119. Which item of Vulcan the blacksmith's clothing arouses Flavia's interest?

120. Why has Vulcan come back to Pompeii?

121. What is strange about grape juice in barrels that is being turned into wine?

122. Vulcan's donkey is called Modestus, because he is humble. If a king rides into a town on a donkey, what does that signify? What if he rides in on a horse?

123. Why is Nubia shocked when Flavia passes Gaius a piece of bread with her left hand?

124. Roman fathers had the right to reject their newborn children without question. Why did Vulcan's father secretly abandon him rather than openly rejecting him?

125. What animals are sacrificed at the Vulcanalia?

126. Apart from the early tremors, what is the first sign of trouble preceding the eruption of Vesuvius? Which of the four friends has had strange premonitions of doom?

127. Roman girls could legally marry from the age of twelve. Who decides to get married in *The Secrets of Vesuvius* and how old is she?

128. What causes the smell that kills the birds in the trees (and has killed animals before), and what does it smell like?

129. As the volcano erupts, where do the detectives and their friends escape to?

130. Why are the people of Pompeii advised to stay in their homes?

For the answers to these questions, turn to page 105.

MUSIC AND MUSICIANS

131. Nubia has some favourite songs she likes to play or sing. Link the song with the person, place or event which inspired it:
    1. 'The Song of the Traveller'   A. The *Myrtilla*
    2. 'The Raven and the Dove'   B. Nubia's father
    3. 'Slave Song'   C. Taharqo
    4. 'Land of White'   D. Chased by dogs
    5. 'Dog Song'   E. Miriam's wedding
    6. 'Sailing Song'   F. Villa Limona
    7. 'The Song of the Maiden'   G. Clio

132. In *The Thieves of Ostia*, how much is the lotus-wood flute Nubia sees in the market on the way to find the harbourmaster?
    A) 10 sesterces
    B) 100 sesterces
    C) 150 sesterces

133. *Volare!* is a popular modern Italian song but it also has a Latin meaning. What does 'volare!' mean? What does 'cantare!' mean?

134. In the first part of *The Pirates of Pompeii*, what instrument does Nubia play?

135. How did Aristo obtain his lyre in *The Pirates of Pompeii*?
    A) He stole it
    B) He bought it
    C) He borrowed it

136. In *The Assassins of Rome*, which musical instrument is used to vanquish the would-be assassin?

137. In Felix's song about the princess Ariadne, on which island did she find love?

138. Nubia's gift with music is first demonstrated when she . . .

    A) Calms the dogs that had been chasing Flavia and Jonathan and herself
    B) Plays a song which makes Flavia's father cry
    C) Charms a snake in the market

139. Which instrument does Felix make a present of to Lupus?

140. What is the name of the instrument Simeon played when he lived in Jerusalem?

141. What is the name of the song Jonathan composes and performs at the Feast of Tabernacles?

142. By posing as musicians, Jonathan and his uncle

hope to gain an audience with whom in *The Assassins of Rome*?

143. In *The Twelve Tasks of Flavia Gemina*, what song is Nubia playing when she realises she loves Aristo?

144. What is the surface covering on Lupus's drum?

145. In *The Assassins of Rome*, Jonathan's uncle Simeon the Zealot sings a song based on Psalm 137 from the Bible, about a tree and a river. What kind of tree is it?

146. In *The Assassins of Rome* Flavia and her friends try to infiltrate the Imperial Palace by pretending to be musicians. What instrument does Sisyphus play?

147. According to Aristo's Scroll, which one of the following is *not* a known instrument?
   1. Tortoiseshell lyre
   2. Lotus-wood flute
   3. Goatskin drum
   4. Syrian barbitron
   5. Jangly tambourine
   6. Breathy pan-pipes
   7. Reeded double-aulos

148. In *The Dolphins of Laurentum*, what does Pliny use to strum his lyre?

149. Who breaks Nubia's flute in *The Pirates of Pompeii*?
    A) Flavia
    B) Pulchra
    C) Lupus

150. Who is Nubia's song 'The Storyteller' based on?
    A) Herself
    B) Aristo
    C) Jonathan

For the answers to these questions, turn to page 106.

THE PIRATES
OF POMPEII

The god of wine, Dionysus, reclines after
changing drowning pirates into dolphins.
*(Illustration based on a Greek
black-figure kylix of around 540 BC)*

151. What is the name of the 'curing plant' that Doctor Mordecai wants the children to find?

152. Who seems to be dying at the start of the book and has a near-death dream calling him or her back to life?

153. What do the professional mourners do to their faces?

154. What is the name of the child Flavia and Nubia find in the cave that the dogs have led them to, and why is she there?

155. What is the element in the water that turns tongues red?

156. By what other name is Kuanto, the leader of the runaway slaves, known?

157. Why is Miriam forced to wear a scarf on her head?

158. In the first century AD, runaway slaves were punished harshly in order to discourage other slaves from absconding. In his conversation with Flavia, Felix mentions two ways in which runaway slaves were punished. What were they?

159. Who is the surprise visitor to the refugee camp on the day after the play?

160. What is Publius Pollius Felix's connection to Flavia's family?

161. Where did Titus serve as a soldier?

162. What does Titus pledge to do for the two thousand refugees?

163. After the destruction of Jerusalem in AD 70, many Jews said God's wrath would fall upon Rome if Titus ever came to power. Why?

164. What animal do the detectives liken Felix to? Who first warned them to be wary of him?

165. What are the names of Felix's three daughters?

166. What is the name of Felix's wife?

167. Where does Pulchra keep her slave, Leda, when she misbehaves?

168. How old is the Greek drinking cup that Felix gives Flavia?

169. What name does Pulchra call Flavia in error?

170. Why didn't Nubia go straight to Flavia after her beating from Pulchra?

171. In Roman times, if pirates kidnapped poor children they could sell them as slaves on the

other side of the empire. What did they often do with captured rich children?

172. Why don't the kidnappers believe Pulchra when she tells them who she is?

173. Where does Kuanto plan to take his band of escaped slaves?

174. Why do the pirates pour cold seawater onto Flavia and Jonathan before leaving them?

175. Nubia meets many runaway slaves in her time away from Flavia. What is the name of the old, educated man who has been forced to work in the vineyards?

176. What is the name of the island off the coast near Surrentum?

177. Nubia means to use sleeping powder to subdue the pirates. What powder is actually used on them?

178. What effect does the wrong powder have on the pirates who take it?

179. What do the detectives find stored in sacks in the hold of the ship which they then use to catch the pirates off-guard?

180. At the end of the book, we learn several new pieces of information about Nubia's past. Which clan do we discover that she belongs to?

For the answers to these questions, turn to page 107.

ANIMALS

181. Which creature steals Captain Geminus's amethyst signet ring at the beginning of the Roman Mysteries series?

182. Which animals does Flavia Gemina encounter in the graveyard while looking for her father's signet ring?

183. What is the name of Gaius Flavius Geminus's dog, and what does its name mean?

184. In *The Secrets of Vesuvius*, what animal does the blacksmith Vulcan ride upon?

185. When Captain Geminus is shipwrecked, he ends up on an island inhabited by what type of animal?

186. The women of Campania believe that first love is the most passionate in a girl's life, as fierce as the bite of a spider-like creature. To cure first love's passion and the poison of the bite they do a dance called the Tarantella, named after this creature. What creature is a tarantella?

187. In *The Dolphins of Laurentum*, which birds wheel in their thousands at dusk?

188. In their household shrines, many Romans had a picture or sculpture of a particular creature they considered lucky. What is this lucky animal?

189. In *The Secrets of Vesuvius*, Aristo finds a scroll by Diodorus of Sicily telling how animals fled a city three days before it was engulfed by the sea. Which animals fled?

190. In *The Assassins of Rome*, four mules pull Feles' delivery cart. Their names come from a famous mosaic in Ostia. Match the name of the mule to its meaning:
    1. Pudes   A. Limping
    2. Podagrosus   B. Mincing
    3. Barosus   C. Tipsy
    4. Potiscus   D. Modest

191. Nubia loves animals. At the beginning of *The Assassins of Rome*, which animals is she closely observing?

192. In *The Assassins of Rome*, what animal does Rizpah give Jonathan to comfort him?

193. In *The Dolphins of Laurentum*, there is a rock in the sea near the site of the sunken treasure. Which birds sit on this rock to dry their wings?

194. In *The Twelve Tasks of Flavia Gemina*, the four children hear that a camelopard is on the loose. What does Nubia later call this animal?

195. In *The Twelve Tasks of Flavia Gemina*, which animals escape being sacrificed at the Temple of Saturn on the first day of the Saturnalia?

For the answers to these questions, turn to page 108.

THE ASSASSINS
OF ROME

Odysseus and his men put out the eye of
the Cyclops, the mythical one-eyed giant.
(Illustration based on a black-figure vase)

196. Among his birthday presents in *The Assassins of Rome*, Jonathan receives an abacus, a cloak and a scroll. What does Pulchra give him?

197. Name two of the three disasters that happened to Jonathan on his past birthdays.

198. Why is the scent of lemon blossom so important to Mordecai ben Ezra?

199. Flavia observes that all four friends have something in common. What is it?

200. What reason does Jonathan's father give for his mother's refusal to leave Jerusalem? Who does Jonathan blame for her deciding to stay?

201. While serving in Judaea, the young commander Titus fell in love with a beautiful Jewish queen ten years older than himself. What was her name?

202. Who is Simeon ben Jonah and what crime is he accused of?

203. What possession of his mother's has Jonathan been forbidden to touch? What item does he take from it?

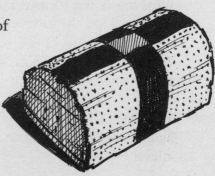

204. Titus sacked the city of Jerusalem. What does 'sack' mean?

205. According to Simeon, why did the residents of Jerusalem run out of food long before Titus's legions expected?

206. After Titus's legions took control of Jerusalem, many slaves were sent to Corinth, to continue Nero's project of cutting a canal through an isthmus. What is an isthmus?

207. Before the capture of Jerusalem, Jonathan's uncle Simeon was a Zealot. What is another name for a Zealot?

208. Where does Lupus end up when he runs away from Jonathan's birthday meal?

209. For what crime is Mordecai ben Ezra arrested and on what evidence?

210. Even though the wax has melted, how can Lupus know what Jonathan's message said in its entirety?

211. What cargo accompanies Nubia and Flavia on their journey to Rome?

212. On which of Rome's seven hills was the Imperial Palace? On which of those seven hills was Nero's Golden House?

213. Which family member does Flavia hope to see on arriving in Rome?

214. As Lupus faces the probability of his death, what are his two big regrets? Who then rescues him?

215. Who offers to help Flavia and Nubia track down Jonathan in Rome?

216. According to Sisyphus, who was Queen Berenice in love with, and what forced the lovers apart?

217. The Ludi Romani was a two-week-long holiday in honour of Jupiter Optimus Maximus. What was the main form of entertainment during the festival?

218. What punishment is Jonathan given when he and Simeon are captured after Domitian's banquet?

219. How does Nubia help Sisyphus to gain 1,000 denarii (4,000 sesterces)?

220. Rizpah is the name of the little girl who leads Jonathan to his mother. What is her mother's name?

221. What colour are the robes worn by the women in the Golden House?

222. The Imperial Palace and Nero's Golden House are connected by a cryptoporticus. What is a cryptoporticus?

223. What do the Jewish women in the Golden House do all day?

224. In Homer's *Odyssey* what was the name of Odysseus's faithful wife, who wove all day and unpicked at night?

225. After the assassins are dealt with, what privilege does Titus confer on Jonathan's entire family?

For the answers to these questions, turn to page 109.

THE ILLUSTRATED
ARISTO'S SCROLL

At the back of each of the Roman Mysteries is a glossary of unfamiliar words, with definitions. Have you ever wondered what these people, places and objects really looked like? Here are pictures of fifteen objects, all of which you'll find in Aristo's scrolls in the first six books in the series. For each picture, can you match its name and also its description from the columns on pages 56-58?

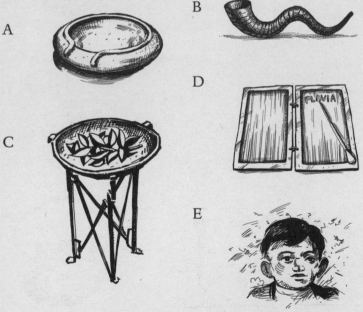

A

B

C

D

E

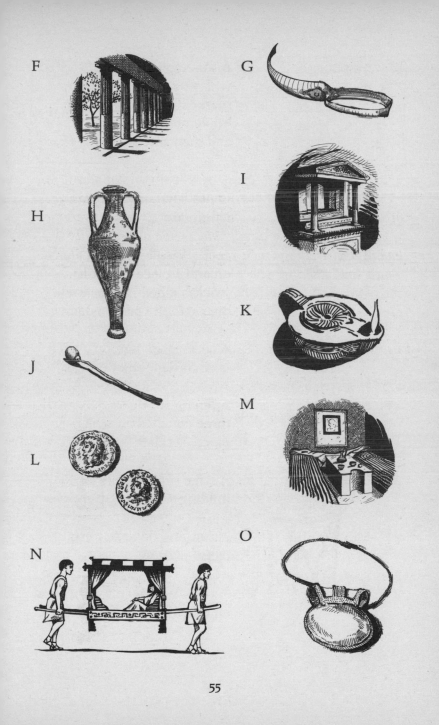

F

G

H

I

J

K

L

M

N

O

226. Amphora	1. A thin tablet of wood coated with wax which can be marked by a sharp implement (stylus) and then smoothed for reuse.
227. Brazier	2. A brass coin worth about £1 in modern terms (though values vary).
228. Bulla	3. A clay vessel filled with olive oil and a piece of string (wick). When lit, the wick burns till the oil runs out.
229. Fresco	4. A soft sea-sponge on a stick used to wipe the bottom.
230. Lararium	5. A dining room, usually with three couches on which diners reclined.
231. Litter	6. A large clay storage jar for holding wine, oil or grain.
232. Moratorium	7. A painting done in fresh, damp plaster.
233. Oil-lamp	8. A columned walkway around an inner garden or courtyard.

234. Peristyle

9. A coal-filled metal bowl on legs, used to heat a room (like an ancient radiator).

235. Sesterces

10. A rough, flat pottery bowl, embedded with grit, for grinding spices, etc.

236. Shofar

11. A bronze scraper for cleaning skin at the baths.

237. Sponge-stick

12. A special trumpet made from a ram's horn. Used to announce Jewish holy days.

238. Strigil and flask

13. A moving chair or pallet carried by two to eight men.

239. Triclinium

14. An amulet of leather or metal worn by freeborn children.

240. Wax tablet

15. A small shrine where household gods were worshipped daily.

For the answers to these questions, turn to page 110.

THE DOLPHINS OF LAURENTUM

Arion is rescued by a dolphin.
*(Illustration based on a Greek black-figure
vase from around 490 BC)*

241. In *The Dolphins of Laurentum* what does Lupus use for a drumstrick – and what is its real use?

242. Where is a sponge-stick stored to keep it clean?

243. To which part of your face would you apply kohl?

244. In ancient Rome the legal age of marriage for a girl was twelve. At what age could a girl be betrothed (promised in marriage)?

245. Jonathan and Flavia have adjacent bedrooms. What's the quickest way to get from one room to the other?

246. How many times do the friends have to knock when they want to slip through the secret entrance?

247. What is the name of the beggar who arrives at the Geminus house at the start of the story?

248. Captain Geminus suffers greatly following the shipwreck. Which part of his body is he in danger of having amputated?

249. Why does Doctor Mordecai send Jonathan and Lupus to the meat market?

250. Name six objects which the bailiffs see on Flavia's dressing table.

251. Ferox has recently been wounded in the chest. What has been the effect of his injuries?

252. What present did Lupus's parents give him on his sixth birthday?

253. Where does Umidus work? What is strange about his appearance when he sleeps?

254. Gamala is renowned as a sicarius. What is a sicarius?

255. Which famous Greek potter made the kylix of Dionysus and the pirates?

256. What are the names of the bankers in the forum who want to repossess Flavia's house?

257. Who offers Captain Geminus a place to recover and sanctuary for his family and friends?

258. What precious object does Flavia ask Jonathan to look after when the bailiffs arrive?

259. Whom does Nubia recognise among the male slaves she sees near the temple in the forum?

260. By what means has Venalicius temporarily acquired his freedom?

261. Pliny has a statue of Perseus, created in the Greek Hellenistic style. What does Jonathan think of this style?

262. What precious cargo of Captain Geminus's lies at the bottom of the sea? What was the cargo of the shipwreck at Laurentum?

263. The floors of the villa at Laurentum have beautiful mosaics featuring sea-creatures on them. What creature is on the floor of Flavia's room?

264. What is the name of the Greek island, famous in antiquity for sponge-diving?

265. According to Lupus, what is the maximum number of dives that should not be exceeded in a day?

266. What is significant about the dream of the fish a slave-girl had which suggests it is an omen?

267. What special invention of Jonathan's should help Lupus with his dive?

268. Why does Lupus resist swimming with dolphins?

269. When the children read Lupus's account of how he lost his tongue, they understand why he is repulsed by a certain creature. Which creature?

270. When Lupus's uncle makes a dying wish, what is the very last word or name he speaks?

For the answers to these questions, turn to page 111.

271. Complete Mordecai ben Ezra's greeting: 'Every .... is an uninvited guest.'

272. In *The Twelve Tasks of Flavia Gemina*, Flavia prays at the Temple of Venus, inspired by a song Miriam often sings. Can you complete the words of the song: 'By the gazelles, O......... of ...., do not awake or arouse .... until it so desires.'

273. Whose dying words were: 'Oh dear, I think I'm becoming a god'?

274. Can you remember the riddle the detectives must solve in *The Secrets of Vesuvius*? *My first letter grieves, my second commands, my third sends, my fourth teaches, and my fifth letter rejoices. The first letter is 'A'. The last is 'E'.* What is the mystery word and what does it mean?

275. Fill in the words missing from Tascius's speech at the Vulcanalia: 'Great Vulcan, protect us against the twin dangers of .... and ....'

276. According to the quote in *The Secrets of Vesuvius*, whom does fortune favour?

277. Match the saying to the person or people:
1. Master of the Universe!   A. Aristo
2. Alas!   B. Lupus
3. Pollux!   C. Captain Geminus
4. By Hercules!   D. Libertus and Felix
5. By Apollo!   E. Sisyphus and Flavia
6. Unghhh!   F. Mordecai
7. Juno!   G. Pulchra
8. Great Neptune's beard!   H. Nubia
9. Great Jupiter's eyebrows! I. Uncle Gaius
10. Great Juno's peacock!   J. Jonathan and Flavia

278. *Novum vetus vinum bibo, novo veteri morbo medeor* is a phrase recited at the Meditrinalia. What does it mean?

279. What does *In vino veritas* mean?

280. What is Flavia's mother-tongue, the language she and her friends speak together?

281. What was the lingua franca (most commonly spoken language) in the Roman Empire in the first century AD?

282. Although Aramaic was the language spoken by most Jews from Judaea in the first century AD, Mordecai prefers his family to speak a different language at home. What is it?

283. Having read the first six Roman Mysteries, you will know some Latin words. Match the expression with its meaning:

1. Salve!   A. Three!
2. Vale!   B. Goodbye!
3. Duo!   C. Hello!
4. Ecce!   D. Behold!
5. Tres!   E. Two!
6. Euge!   F. Six!
7. Sex!   G. Hurray!

284. Who proclaims 'You've cried with our music, now laugh with our comedy!' and what play is he or she referring to?

285. Who says that marrying for love is always a bad idea?

286. In *The Twelve Tasks of Flavia Gemina*, Flavia reflects that she likes a drink she can ....?

287. When Flavia and Pulchra have a girl-fight in *The Pirates of Pompeii*, Pulchra calls Flavia a 'Peasant!' What does Flavia call Pulchra in return?

288. Who sees Aristo 'very kissing' in the woods?

289. In *The Pirates of Pompeii*, where does Jonathan tell the boy named Apollo to sit?

290. Who calls Flavia's father 'Captain Square-Jaw' in *The Twelve Tasks of Flavia Gemina*?

For the answers to these questions, turn to page 112.

291. Which one of these items did Perseus *not* use in his quest for the head of Medusa?
    A. A sharp sword
    B. A mirrored shield
    C. Winged sandals
    D. Helmet of invisibility
    E. Potion to protect him from fire
    F. Bag to put her head in afterwards
    G. The eyeball of a witch

292. Who is Cerberus?

293. Who is the God of the Sea?

294. What is Vulcan the god of?

295. According to Aristo, what parts of Vulcan's body were damaged when his mother Juno hurled him from Mount Olympus?

296. Who raised Vulcan after he was thrown from Mount Olympus?

297. The word 'volcano' comes from the god of forges and fire. What is his name?

298. Who is Venus?

299. What was the name of Thetis's real son, for whom Vulcan forged armour?

300. To Nubia, Aristo resembles the god of heralds, merchants and bankers. Who is this god?

301. The Roman god of wine, Bacchus, is often shown as jolly and fat, whereas his Greek equivalent is handsome and dangerous. What is the name of the Greek god of wine?

302. Why is Dionysus linked to dolphins?

303. When Dinoysus was captured by pirates, what animal did he turn himself into?

304. Which King of Tyre carved a sculpture of his ideal woman and then fell in love with his own creation?

305. According to Aristo, why didn't the sea-nymph Amphitrite want to kiss Neptune?

306. How did Neptune honour his official messenger, Delphinus, after he died?

307. When sailors like Captain Geminus survived a shipwreck, they cut off their hair and dedicated it as a thanks offering at the temple of which god?

308. Hercules had to perform twelve 'impossible' tasks to atone for a terrible murder. Whom did he kill?

309. There is at least one Greek myth embedded in each of the Roman Mysteries. Match the myth to the story.

1. *The Thieves of Ostia*	A.	Dionysus and the Pirates
2. *The Secrets of Vesuvius*	B.	Arion of Corinth
3. *The Pirates of Pompeii*	C.	The Labours of Hercules
4. *The Assassins of Rome*	D.	Return of Vulcan to Olympus
5. *The Dolphins of Laurentum*	E.	Odysseus and Penelope
6. *The Twelve Tasks of Flavia Gemina*	F.	Cerberus the three-headed hound

310. Grain is Ostia's lifeblood. Who is the goddess of that substance?

311. Hercules took the world on his shoulders so that which Titan could bring him the golden apples of the Hesperides?

312. What sort of creature did Arion ride? What instrument did he play so beautifully?

313. A fresco in one room of Nero's Golden House shows Odysseus giving a cup of wine to a Cyclops. What is the name of the Cyclops?

314. In the story of Arion and the dolphins, who was the king of Corinth?

315. Hippomenes won whose hand and heart by throwing golden apples?

For the answers to these questions, turn to page 113.

THE TWELVE TASKS OF FLAVIA GEMINA

Hercules performs his sixth
labour by killing the Stymphalian birds.

(Illustration based on a black-figure vase from around 545 BC)

316. In *The Twelve Tasks of Flavia Gemina* what special event at Jonathan's house precedes the Saturnalia?

317. Flavia and her friends have recently helped solve a case of theft at a bakery. Who owns the bakery?

318. Flavia dreams that Hercules tells her to go on a quest. The next day she sees a fresco painter in her dining room. Why does she believe his presence is a confirmation of her dream?

319. A ship from Alexandria carrying beasts for the arena has been delayed by storms and, when it docks, the ravenous animals escape. Flavia calls one of them a Stymphalian bird. What is it really?

320. What is the name of the escaped lion and what is the name of his trainer?

321. What is a venefica?

322. Why does Captain Geminus forbid Flavia from leaving the house?

323. Some of the little dolls Jonathan sees being sold as Saturnalia gifts are likenesses of real people. Can you name two such people?

324. Which one of the following was *not* one of Hercules's tasks?
    1. Bring back the head of Medusa
    2. Kill the Nemean lion

3. Clean the Augean stables
4. Catch a deer
5. Bring back the Amazon queen's belt
6. Catch a fierce boar
7. Kill the Stymphalian birds

325. The wise woman of Ostia was born in the year Octavian became the Emperor Augustus. This makes her over one hundred years old. One of her nicknames means 'old woman' in Latin. What is it?

326. What is different about the appearance of Vibia, Cartilia's mother, on Flavia's second visit?

327. Nubia loves to go to the public baths in winter because she can get warm. Which one of the following rooms would she not like in December?
1. Caldarium
2. Laconicum
3. Sudatorium
4. Tepidarium
5. Frigidarium
6. Solarium
7. Apodyterium

328. What is the name of the gladiator whom Doctor Mordecai treats – and what is the reason for the treatment?

329. How did Hercules clear out King Augeus's stables without immersing himself in the muck?

330. According to a stablehand, what do the ladies of Ostia pay a gold coin for a bottle of – and what do they do with it?

331. In her note to Aristo, where does Diana suggest they meet – and when?

332. What is the name of the mythical master who fed chopped-up people to horses, and also the priest of Mithras?

333. Which of the detectives' pets is injured by the ostrich?

334. How would you recognise an Amazon woman from her clothing?

335. The Wise Woman of Ostia claims that most of the evil in the world comes from two sources – what are they?

336. What did Diana do to herself take when she learned that Aristo did not love her?

337. What does Flavia learn about Cartilia's husband?

338. How do the friends demonstrate their appreciation of the oysters Pliny has sent?

339. Christmas today has many similarities with the Roman Saturnalia. Name the one which Flavia and her friends would *not* recognise.

1. Lighting extra candles and lights
2. Feasting
3. Drinking
4. Greenery around the house
5. Giving gifts
6. Sleigh pulled by reindeer
7. Wearing replica crowns
8. Games and gambling
9. Mottoes and sayings
10. Colourful conical hats

340. What is the name of Captain Geminus's potential bride?

341. What power does the King of the Saturnalia have during the five days of the festival?

342. How is the King of the Saturnalia chosen?

343. Who finishes painting the fresco in the Geminus household?

344. What calamity befalls many of the inhabitants of Ostia, including Flavia?

345. What is the most notable feature of the weather on the day of the special event at the end of the book?

For the answers to these questions, turn to page 114 .

THE NUMBERS QUIZ

346. In *The Dolphins of Laurentum*, Lupus sees Gamala, whose whipmarks show he has been punished for a terrible crime. How many lash wounds does Lupus count on Gamala's back?

347. A dowry was a Roman wife's financial security. In *The Twelve Tasks of Flavia Gemina*, how many gold coins are sewn into Miriam's betrothal headscarf?

348. Solve this equation in Roman numerals: XLIV + LXVI = ...?

349. The gold coin called an aureus is worth how many sesterces?

350. When she first meets Flavia, Nubia wears a wooden plaque below her iron collar with six Cs on it. What amount does this represent?

351. When old debts are called in by the bankers, how much money must Captain Geminus pay to prevent his possessions being seized?

352. What is the reserve price of each of the African male slaves in *The Dolphins of Laurentum*?

353. Solve this equation in Roman numerals: XCIX + I
= ....

354. How far down at the bottom of the sea is the
wreck of the ship in *The Dolphins of Laurentum*.
A) Sixty feet. B) Eighty feet. C) One hundred feet.

355. After several attempts over two days, for how
many beats can Lupus hold his breath underwater
in *The Dolphins of Laurentum*?

356. Can you match these life dates to a real-life person
you will know from the Roman Mysteries?
1. 106-43 BC   A. Titus (Emperor of Rome)
2. 70-19 BC   B. Admiral Pliny (writer, sea
                   captain, etc)
3. AD 39-81   C. Virgil (famous Latin poet)
4. AD 23-79   D. Vespasian (Emperor of Rome)
5. AD 9-79   E. Cicero (Rome's greatest orator)

357. Solve this equation in Roman numerals: XX +
XXX = ...

358. How long did the Trojan war last? How long did it
take Odysseus to return home? For how many
years was he away from Ithaca in all?

359. On which day of the month are the Ides of
March, May, July and October?

360. In Flavia's time, how many days did the Saturnalia
last?

361. The Romans used to count the hours of the day from dawn. If dawn was 6 am, what would the fifth and eleventh hours have been?

362. When Nubia plays her flute, she names each of the polished holes beneath her fingertips after a member of her family – so she plays a mother-note, a father-note, and so on. How many people does she remember in this special way?

363. How old did boys have to be before they are allowed to wear the pure white garment known as a toga virilis?

364. Although this rule wasn't often enforced, how old must a slave have been in ancient Roman times before he or she could be freed?

365. Solve this equation in Roman numerals: M – CCC = ...

For the answers to these questions, turn to page 115.

GLORIOUS FOOD

Featuring Questions by
Guest Quizmaster Roisin Corbett

366. What is Doctor Mordecai's cure-all?

367. The Romans had a saying 'From the egg to the apple', meaning from the beginning of the meal to the end. When Flavia and her friends dine with Admiral Pliny, they start with eggs and finish with apples. What do they have in between?

368. On the Vulcanalia what do people offer as a substitute for their own lives?

369. What does Nubia say the magnesium water tasted like?

370. Which fruits hang from the roof in Jonathan's succah?

371. What are the ingredients of Lupus's special meal for divers?

372. Why does Lupus put vinegar on his oysters?

373. What food does Rizpah give Jonathan to eat in the Golden House, and what is its particular flavour?

374. As King of the Saturnalia, Flavia commands her friends to name their favourite foods. Match the favourite foods to the characters, as they appear in *The Twelve Tasks of Flavia Gemina*:

1. Flavia	A. Roast lamb
2. Jonathan	B. Dates
3. Mordecai	C. Roast chicken
4. Nubia	D. Mushrooms
5. Lupus	E. Oysters
6. Aristo	F. Salted tuna
7. Captain Geminus	G. Venison stew

375. What food does Jonathan memorably try for the first time in *The Pirates of Pompeii*?

376. In *The Secrets of Vesuvius*, what complimentary snack do the four detectives get with their wine at the tavern in Pompeii?

377. In *The Twelve Tasks of Flavia Gemina*, Alma is worried that Flavia will use too much of which expensive spice?

378. In *The Dolphins of Laurentum*, during the meal where the friends first entertain the younger Pliny, what two unusual ingredients are in the omelette?

379. What locally-caught delicacy does young Pliny serve the friends when they first dine at his Laurentine Villa?

380. At the beginning of *The Assassins of Rome*, Flavia

asks Jonathan if the cup is half full or half empty. What is in the cup?

381. Which one of the following did Romans *not* have:
     1. Knives
     2. Forks
     3. Spoons
     4. Plates
     5. Napkins
     6. Glass cups
     7. Toothpicks

382. In *The Twelve Tasks of Flavia Gemina* which food was the love-potion mixed in with?

383. In *The Assassins of Rome*, what extremely exotic food was being enjoyed at a dinner party of the Emperor's younger brother Domitian?

384. In *The Twelve Tasks of Flavia Gemina* what food did Flavia bring Cartilia as a Saturnalia present?

385. Which one of the following foods did Romans *not* consume:
     1. Snails fried in garlic oil
     2. Stuffed dormice
     3. Sauce made of fish-entrails
     4. Chocolate-covered ants
     5. Chopped sows' udders
     6. Whole little birds
     7. Wine mixed with perfume

For the answers to these questions, turn to page 116.

386. What is the name of Captain Geminus's ship – and who is it named after?

387. What is the name of the ship on which Avitus, the suspect in *The Thieves of Ostia*, sails?

388. Why is the *Vespa* notorious?

389. How are the ships of the Roman Imperial Fleet powered?

390. What colour are the sails on the pirates' ship in *The Pirates of Pompeii*?

391. In *The Dolphins of Laurentum* what name does the new owner of the *Vespa* give it?

392. How do the oars of a merchant ship differ from warships?

393. What is the name of the mythical whirlpool near Sicily that could destroy entire ships?

394. Who was Thetis?

395. Why does the fisherman Robur object to the presence of the dolphins in the waters off Laurentum?

396. What animal was sacrificed for the purification of a ship?

397. Where on the Bay of Naples was part of the Roman fleet stationed in AD 79?

398. From which port was Nubia taken by ship to Ostia?

399. Which one of the following was *not* considered a bad omen on board ship?
   1. Stepping onto the ship with your left foot
   2. Sneezing
   3. Owls
   4. Embarking on an even numbered day
   5. Getting your hair cut
   6. Forgetting to sacrifice to the gods
   7. Cats

400. Which one of the following Roman towns did *not* have a port or harbour in Flavia's time?
   1. Ostia
   2. Stabia

3. Pompeii
4. Misenum
5. Capua
6. Ravenna
7. Puteoli

401. Phoenicians were renowned as sailors in Roman times. Captain Geminus has three on his crew. They are brothers. Two are named Quartus and Quintus. What is the third one called?

402. Captain Geminus also has a crewmember called Ebenus. Where is he from?

403. What did Romans use to seal the planks of the ship?

404. When a sleek, low warship passes the *Myrtilla* on its way to Misenum, what is the officer doing to help the rowers keep the rhythm?

405. What did Greeks and Romans often paint on the prows of their warships?

For the answers to these questions, turn to page 117.

THE NAME GAME

*In the Roman Mysteries, the Latin names
often have hidden meanings. Can you identify
the meanings of the following names?*

406. Flavius/Flavia means
   A. Tasty
   B. Tawny
   C. Teacher

407. Geminus/Gemina means
   A. Twin
   B. Jewel
   C. Grubby

408. Lupus means
   A. Wolf
   B. Tiger
   C. Horse

409. Alma means
   A. Mother
   B. Cook
   C. Nurse

410. Caudex means
   A. Doorkeeper
   B. Blockhead
   C. Cow-like

411. Libertus means
A. Freedman
B. Writer
C. Torch-bearer

412. Venalicius means
A. Villain
B. Slave-dealer
C. One-eyed

413. Anus means
A. Old woman
B. Female donkey
C. One-eyed

414. Lusca means
A. Pretty
B. Soapy
C. One-eyed

415. Felix means
A. Cat-like
B. Dog-like
C. Lucky

416. Aurarius means
A. Goldsmith
B. Silversmith
C. Blacksmith

417. Vespa means
A. Small motorcycle

B. Big motorcycle
C. Wasp

418. Feles means
    A. Lion
    B. Tiger
    C. Cat

419. Tigris means
    A. Lion
    B. Tiger
    C. Cat

420. Hariola means
    A. Bean-fed
    B. Egyptian
    C. Soothsayer

421. Scuto means
    A. Sword
    B. Shield
    C. Companion

422. Taurus means
    A. Tourist
    B. Tower
    C. Bull

423. Gutta means
    A. Drainpipe
    B. Spotty
    C. Fatty

424. Fimus means
   A. Dung
   B. Clay
   C. Hay

425. Fuscus means
   A. Dark
   B. Dangerous
   C. Celery

426. Robur means
   A. Robber
   B. Oak
   C. Radish

427. Bulbus means
   A. Baldy
   B. Fatty
   C. Onion

428. Alga means
   A. Nursemaid
   B. Seaweed
   C. Carrot

429. Pulchra means
   A. Posh
   B. Beautiful
   C. Parsnip

430. Oleosus means
   A. Oily

B. Oleander
C. Onion

431. Umidus means
   A. Damp
   B. Bean-fed
   C. Wide-eyed

432. Frustilla means
   A. Frustrated
   B. Ancient
   C. Crumbs

433. Rosa means
   A. Beady
   B Red
   C. Rose

434. Myrtilla means
   A. Mother
   B. Ship
   C. Myrtle

435. Rufus means
   A. Red-haired
   B. Wrestler
   C. Burly

For the answers to these questions, turn to page 117.

With contributions from Roman Mysteries fans
S.R.H. James, Roisin Corbett and Pekka Tuomisto

436. What is the name of the street on which Flavia, Nubia, Jonathan and Lupus live?

437. What do Jonathan and Admiral Pliny have in common?

438. The kidnappers Actius, Sorex, and Lucrio are real names from Pompeian graffiti. According to the graffiti, what was their profession?

439. What is Nubia's real name?

440. Simeon was sent to kill someone in Nero's Golden House. What were the names of the other two assassins?

441. Before Venalicius became a slave-dealer, what was his profession?

442. Which one of the following was not a traditional gift during the Saturnalia?
A. Little Dolls
B. Silver objects
C. Chocolates
D. Candles

E. Oil-lamps
F. Food
G. Money

443. What is a 'urinator'?

444. Match the Roman word with the room of the house:
1. Vestibule   A. Rainwater pool
2. Triclinium   B. Bedroom
3. Tablinum   C. Study
4. Impluvium   D. Entryway
5. Compluvium   E. Dining room
6. Atrium   F. Reception room often with pool
7. Cubiculum   G. Skylight above pool

445. What kind of weather do Romans expect when the Dog Star is in the sky?

446. In *The Assassins of Rome*, why can't Feles enter Rome until after dark?

447. Which white, pyramid-shaped monument tells travellers from Ostia that they are almost at Rome?

448. What is unusual about the dining-room in Pliny's Laurentine villa?

449. Why does the trickle of plaster dust from the ceiling of a Roman apartment block alarm Jonathan?

450. Which bull-necked emperor was known as the Mule-Driver?

451. In the Temple of Rome and Augustus in Ostia's forum, Rome is depicted as a statue of an Amazon with her foot on a ball. What does the ball represent?

452. Why do fresco-painters have to work fast?

453. Listening to music gives the Emperor Titus relief from what physical ailment?

454. The great Flavian amphitheatre was built by Vespasian with money and slaves obtained from the destruction of Jerusalem. What is this amphitheatre called today?

455. Ostia's Forum of the Corporations was where different groups of people met to socialise and do business. Which one of the following groups certainly did *not* meet there?

1. Exotic beast importers
2. Olive oil importers
3. Rope and sail-makers
4. Tanners
5. Grain measurers
6. Vestal virgins
7. Ship-owners

456. The vigiles were a cohort of soldiers on a posting from Rome. They had barracks in Ostia and patrolled the town in pairs. What two things did they vigilantly look out for while patrolling?

457. What would you do with a dithyramb?

458. What is traditionally mixed during the festival of the Meditrinalia?

459. Who are the Capitoline triad?

460. What is the name of the strange phenomenon of light that is also known as 'cold fire'?

461. Felix's opulent villa is a few miles south of Surrentum. What is Surrentum known as today?

462. From which language do the words 'necropolis' and 'peristyle' come?

463. A freed slave took on his master's first name (*praenomen*) and surname (*nomen gentilicum*) and

kept his slave-name as his third name (*cognomen*).
What was Phrixus's new name after he was freed
by his young master Pliny?

464. In which scroll (book) of the *Aeneid* does Aeneas
meet Cerberus?

465. What are ludi?

466. What does an aqueduct carry?

467. For what does IMP stand?

468. Who is the young Roman god of love?

469. How would you count up to six in Latin?

470. What is the singular of denarii?

471. Two broad vertical stripes on a tunic – one either
side of the neckline – show the man wearing it is
a patrician. What class of men wear tunics with
two narrow stripes?

472. What is the holiest and most solemn day in the Jewish calendar, when Jews fast for twenty-four hours to atone for their sins?

473. What is the Hebrew word for 'peace', which can also be used as a greeting of 'hello' or 'goodbye'?

474. According to Rizpah, what was Nero's original use for the large octagonal room in his Golden House?

475. Some Roman houses had a mosaic of a fierce dog near their front door. Sometimes the Latin phrase *cave canem* was written in mosaic chips beneath the dog. What does *cave canem* mean?

476. In *The Dolphins of Laurentum*, Nubia sees some muscular young men being sold as slaves in Ostia's forum. Later she learns they have all been sent to a special school in Capua. What kind of a school was it?

477. According to Flavia, which emperor wore five tunics in winter, to keep warm?

478. Who famously cheated in order to be elected King of the Saturnalia, even though he was already the most powerful man in the Roman Empire?

479. In Flavia's time, which god's birthday was celebrated on December 25th?

480. What item of clothing did people wear on the Saturnalia to show they were 'free' from the usual restrictions?

481. Who is Alma?

482. Why does Vesuvius look so green?

483. What is the name of Ostia's junior magistrate (first met in *The Thieves of Ostia*)?

484. Who is Domitian?

485. What kind of rock, connected to grooming in the Roman Mysteries, is light enough to float?

For the answers to these questions, turn to page 118.

NUBIA-ISMS

Nubia's Latin is not yet fluent and she unintentionally says some strange things. Match what Nubia says with what is meant.

486.	fox fur essence	A.	Someone who sees the worst
487.	muntulumpus	B.	What Lupus's father was
488.	rude brick	C.	Wealth
489.	sassassin	D.	Home of the gods
490.	neronpopeye	E.	An emperor and his lover
491.	low dead dies	F.	What Lupus uses to cheat
492.	sessimisp	G.	Luminous plankton
493.	spongy-diver	H.	Writing in red letters
494.	immorality	I.	The state of living forever
495.	Divity Eye	J.	A hired killer

OUTTAKES

Each of the following passages never made it into the final version. Can you guess which of the first six Roman Mysteries each came from?

496. 'I like the Saturnalia,' said Flavia Gemina as she peeled a grape for her door-slave Caudex. 'Everything's back to front and upside down.'

Caudex nodded as he accepted the grape. He chewed it carefully, then swallowed. The big slave was wearing his best tunic and sandals. He reclined awkwardly on a dining couch near a hot brazier.

497. 'Flavia,' said Nubia, 'why does your father and your uncle always killing things.'

'Well, they have to make sacrifices to keep the gods happy. Pater has to make sacrifices for a safe journey. And I think Uncle Gaius wanted to know if it's a good day to look for a new house.'

'But why do the gods want sacrifice? Do they eat the chicken?'

'No. I think they like the blood. And the smell. And sometimes you can tell the future from the chicken's insides.'

498. Lupus was stunned with boredom. As Pliny droned on, reciting the fourth scroll of his epic poem, Lupus saw Flavia stifle a yawn. Jonathan

had his eyes closed, as if he were concentrating.
He didn't fool Lupus. Nubia, on the other hand,
seemed interested and alert. She was staring at the
ceiling. Followed her gaze, Lupus saw a gecko
stuff a long-legged insect into his grinning mouth.
The gecko looked happy. He obviously didn't
understand Latin.

499. Although Flavia usually stayed to watch until the
Myrtilla passed right out of sight, Nubia was still
shivering with fear, so Flavia decided to take her
home quickly. Her father was a diminishing figure
at the helm, busy with the two large paddles
which steered the ship, but just before she turned
to go, Flavia saw him wave one last time.

500. Jonathan smiled and muttered through clenched
teeth: 'What do you do when you meet an
Emperor?'
'I'm not sure,' whispered Flavia. 'I think you kiss
his hand.'
But when the Emperor stood before them,
Nubia surprised them all. She clapped softly five
times, dipping her head and bending her knees a
little more with each clap.
Titus smiled down at her: 'Charming.'

501. Jonathan said, 'We should make up animal names
for ourselves, too, like Lupus. I'd like to be called
Ursus, the bear. I like bears because they can
be fierce but also funny. I saw one in the
forum once. He danced for his master and

did tricks. Also, bears like honey, and so do I.'

Flavia thought for a few moments and then said, 'I'll be an owl, because my father calls me his little owl and the owl is Minerva's bird.'

'Who is Minerva?' asked Nubia, who had only been in Italia for a few weeks.

ANSWERS

MAP QUIZZES

OSTIA IN AD 79
1. Roman Gate - D
2. Marina Gate - A
3. Flavia's house - G
4. Temple of Hercules - F
5. Laurentum Gate - H
6. Forum of the Corporations - C
7. Theatre - L
8. Avita's Grave - B
9. Temple of Rome and Augustus - E
10. Synagogue - K

GAIUS'S FARM
11. Impluvium - E
12. Latrine - G
13. Stables - K
14. Slaves' quarters - A
15. Library - H
16. Portico - C
17. Atrium - L
18. Toolshed - B
19. Wine cellar - D
20. Well - F

21. Appian Way - E
22. Pyramid of Cestius - D
23. Flaminian Way - H
24. Golden House - A
25. Circus Maximus - L
26. Capitoline Hill - F
27. River Tiber - K
28. Roman Forum - G
29. Imperial Palace - C
30. Colossus - B

THE THIEVES OF OSTIA

31. Ides of June (13th), AD 79.
32. It was a gift from his late wife, Flavia's mother.
33. Castor and Pollux.
34. My little owl.
35. City of the dead or graveyard.
36. Decumanus Maximus.
37. One horrible blind eye. Rotten teeth. Hairy nostrils. Missing ear.
38. Burning Rome.
39. Six hundred sesterces.
40. Inviting your slave to recline means you are granting him or her freedom.
41. 1.C, 2.D, 3.E, 4.B, 5.A.
42. Flavia's father's patron.
43. Three years old.
44. Bobas.
45. None.
46. Hydrophobia.

47. A monkey.

48. The lowest possible score thrown on a dice.

49. Coloured wax.

50. To find out about Avitus, who works on boats.

51. The synagogue.

52. You sit down on the ground.

53. Avitus.

54. They run alone.

55. Gold coins.

56. A dolphin.

57. Cerberus.

58. Vegetable dye.

59. Vespasian.

60. Tiger.

CLOTHES AND FASHION

61. Publius Avitus Proculus wearing a pale yellow tunic.

62. 1.G, 2.A, 3.E, 4.F, 5.C, 6.D, 7.B.

63. Sour wine and pine resin.

64. B) A lavender stola.

65. 1.D, 2.B, 3.H, 4.G, 5.C, 6.F, 7.A, 8.E.

66. Pink ribbons.

67. Lupus and Jonathan.

68. A) Purple toga.

69. He was wearing a winter toga in the summer.

70. B) Cone shaped.

71. Dolphins.

72. A) Wool from a goat's stomach.

73. B) A white robe, a saffron yellow cloak, a bright orange veil.

74. The club of Hercules.

75. 1B, 2A, 3C.
76. It has only one sleeve, leaving the right arm and shoulder free.
77. 1.B, 2.C, 3.D, 4.F, 5.G, 6.H, 7.E, 8.A
78. The toga.
79. 6 ties.
80. 4 sundial wristwatches.

WRITERS AND WRITINGS

81. The Torah.
82. Twelve.
83. It is minuscule.
84. A manual on how to throw javelin from horseback.
85. Pliny's *Natural History*.
86. Stylus.
87. 2. Paper (it was unknown in Roman times).
88. Virgil.
89. He used perfume, which made the dolphin sick.
90. Decimus and his father.
91. Euripides.
92. Apollodorus.
93. Catullus.
94. Song of Songs (or Song of Solomon).
95. Statius.
96. Jesus Christ (whose sayings were not all written down at this time but would have been known and repeated).
97. A portable inkpot which hangs on a chain around his neck.
98. VOLCAN (he is trying to write 'Vulcan').
99. It's easier to take notes as his slave reads to him.
100. Kalends.

101. Roman legions were marching to besiege it.

102. Lupus.

103. His brother's farm between Pompeii and Stabia.

104. It belongs to the slave-ship Vespa.

105. A wasp. It frightened Pliny's slave, whose hysterical flailing upturned the boat.

106. 1.D, 2.C, 3..A, 4.B.

107. To a 'treasure beyond imagining'.

108. Because the fountains constantly overflow to wash away sewerage and other debris.

109. Gaius – by ten minutes.

110. The space behind the figures is painted black, so they show up red-orange. The facial details are then added with a fine brush.

111. A mythological creature half man and half goat.

112. He is holding a hammer and tongs and his deformed legs look too small for his body.

113. He loved Myrtilla, who preferred a ship's captain to a farmer.

114. 24 August AD 79.

115. Midday.

116. A tree fort.

117. They're all named after the nine muses and are all adopted.

118. 6. Historia.

119. He wears a strangely-shaped boot on his right foot.

120. To find the parents who abandoned him at birth.

121. It makes a bubbling, groaning noise.

122. A king comes in peace on a donkey, but intending war

on a horse.

123. Where Nubia comes from, it would be an insult, for the left hand is used to wipe your bottom.

124. He didn't want to upset his wife.

125. Fish.

126. All the animals flee towards the sea. Jonathan dreamed of Jerusalem.

127. Miriam, 'only just turned fourteen'.

128. Sulphur, which smells like rotten eggs.

129. They head for Stabia.

130. Because the tremors are not serious (according to the magistrate) and looters may move in.

MUSIC AND MUSICIANS

131 1.B, 2.G, 3.F, 4.E, 5.D, 6.A, 7.C.

132. B) 100 sesterces.

133. 'To fly!' and 'To sing!'

134. A lotus-wood flute.

135. C) He borrowed it.

136. A tambourine.

137. Naxos.

138. A) Calms the dogs that had been chasing her, Flavia and Jonathan.

139. A drum.

140. The psaltery.

141. 'Penelope's Loom'.

142. The Emperor, Titus.

143. 'Slave Song'.

144. Goat-skin.

145. A willow tree.

146. A gourd filled with lentils.

147. 4. Syrian barbitron.

148. A small ivory wand.

149. B) Pulchra.

150. B) Aristo.

THE PIRATES OF POMPEII

151. Neapolitan cyclamen, or 'amulet'.

152. Jonathan.

153. They scratch their cheeks.

154. Julia, who is five. She is hiding from the kidnappers.

155. Iron.

156. Fuscus.

157. Her hair caught fire when Vesuvius erupted.

158. Crucifixion and execution in the amphitheatre.

159. The Emperor, Titus.

160. He is one of Flavia's uncle's patrons.

161. Judaea.

162. To compensate them for their losses, even if he has to provide the money himself.

163. Titus was the commander of the legions who destroyed Jerusalem and the Temple.

164. A spider. Petrus, the innkeeper said, 'Be careful of the spider and his web.'

165. Polla, known as Pulchra, and Pollina and Pollinilla.

166. Polla Argentaria.

167. A large cedar chest in her room.

168. Over 600 years old.

169. Fulvia.

170. She thought Flavia had called her 'stupid'.

171. They demanded a ransom.

172. After her fight with Flavia, she appears dishevelled.

Also, she was not wearing her usual elegant clothes.

173. The great city of Alexandria in Greece.

174. As punishment – as the thongs dried the salt would cause them to tighten, cutting into the skin.

175. Socrates.

176. Caprea (modern Capri).

177. Mushroom powder.

178. It gives them hallucinations so they think the ship's ropes look like deadly cobras.

179. Chickpeas.

180. The leopard.

ANIMALS

181. Magpie.

182. A pack of angry dogs.

183. Ferox – it means 'ferocious'.

184. A donkey.

185. Birds.

186. A tarantula.

187. Starlings.

188. A snake.

189. Rats, snakes and weasels.

190. 1.D, 2.A, 3.B, 4.C.

191. Four ants.

192. A grey kitten.

193. Cormorants.

194. A giraffe.

195. Some piglets.

THE ASSASSINS OF ROME

196. An expensive alabastron, containing lemon blossom scent.

197. He shot his sister with an arrow, he fell out of a tree, he stepped on a bee.

198. It was the scent his wife, Susannah, used to wear.

199. They believe they don't have mothers.

200. Her father was a priest and he deemed it unseemly for her to leave. Jonathan blames himself.

201. Berenice.

202. Jonathan and Miriam's uncle – their mother's brother. He is accused of being an assassin.

203. Her jewellery box, from which he takes her signet ring.

204. To kill the city's defenders, carry off valuable objects and enslave the inhabitants.

205. Some of the residents destroyed the grain stores, believing it would force their fellow citizens to break out and fight the Romans.

206. A narrow strip of land between water.

207. A freedom fighter. The zealots violently resisted Roman rule.

208. Ensnared in a boar trap.

209. Harbouring an assassin. Strands of Simeon's hair were found in the hearth.

210. It was a new tablet, so the words were the only ones scratched in the wood beneath the wax.

211. Oranges.

212. The Palatine Hill. The Oppian (or Esquiline) Hill.

213. Her aunt – Myrtilla's sister – Lady Cynthia Caecilia.

214. Not knowing if Clio survived the eruption of Vesuivus,

and being unable to avenge his parents' murder. He is rescued by Aristo.

215. Sisyphus, her uncle's secretary.

216. Titus. Being from the East, the Romans were suspicious of her and would not permit Titus to have her as his Queen. He had to choose between duty and love, and he chose duty.

217. Chariot races.

218. He is branded on the arm and sent to work in the latrines.

219. She gives him tips at the races.

220. Rachel.

221. Black.

222. A secret corridor, often underground.

223. They weave.

224. Penelope.

225. Roman citizenship.

THE ILLUSTRATED ARISTO'S SCROLL

226. 6.H

227. 9.C

228. 14.O

229. 7.E

230. 15.I

231. 13.N

232. 10.A

233. 3.K

234. 8.F

235. 2.L

236. 12.B

237. 4. J

238. 11.G
239. 5.M
240. 1.D

THE DOLPHINS OF LAURENTUM

241. A sponge-stick, which is used for wiping your bottom after going to the toilet.
242. In a jar of vinegar.
243. Around the eyes.
244. At any age.
245. Through the secret entrance Jonathan and Lupus have created by removing plaster and bricks from the walls.
246. Four.
247. Captain Geminus.
248. His feet.
249. To get maggots in order to treat Captain Geminus's infected feet.
250. Wooden comb, bath-set, oil-lamp, scent-bottle, bead necklace, make-up box, hairpins of brass, ivory and bone.
251. It has made him gentle.
252. A pig-skin ball.
253. The Baths of Thetis. He sleeps with open eyes, as if he is dead.
254. He is an assassin. Sicarius is the name of the elite Jewish assassination squad. A captured sicarius would be crucified.
255. Exekias.
256. Rufus and Dexter.
257. Pliny the younger at his house at Laurentum.
258. The elegant Greek kylix given to her by Felix.
259. Her eldest brother, Taharqo.

260. Bribery.

261. It's quite overdramatic and 'gaudy'.

262. Spices. Gold.

263. A seahorse.

264. Symi.

265. Seven.

266. The fish had no heart. The fish was called 'lupus'.

267. A float-rope.

268. He thinks it makes him weak, and might distract him from his vow to get revenge.

269. Octopus.

270. Rose.

QUIPS AND QUOTATIONS

271. Stranger.

272. Daughters of Jerusalem. Love.

273. Emperor Vespasian.

274. Asine, which means jackass. See Scroll V of *The Secrets of Vesuvius*.

275. Flame and water.

276. The brave.

277. 1.F, 2.H, 3.J, 4.D, 5.A, 6.B, 7.G, 8.C, 9.I, 10.E.

278. I drink new and old wine, and am healed of new and old disease.

279. In wine there is truth.

280. Latin.

281. Greek.

282. Hebrew.

283. 1.C, 2.B, 3.E, 4.D, 5.A, 6.G, 7.F.

284. Lucrio, as he introduces the play 'The Pirates of Pompeii'.

285. Alma.

286. Chew.

287. 'Harpy!'

288. Nubia.

289. 'With the kids from Oplontis'.

290. Cartilia's ex-husband, Postumus Sergius Caldus.

MYTHS AND LEGENDS

291. E) Potion to protect him from fire.

292. The hound who guards the gates of the Underworld.

293. Neptune.

294. Blacksmiths and metalworkers. He is also a god of sea and fire.

295. His feet and legs.

296. The sea-nymph Thetis.

297. Vulcan.

298. The goddess of love.

299. Achilles.

300. Mercury.

301. Dionysus.

302. Because when some pirates kidnapped him, he changed them into dolphins.

303. He turned into a lion.

304. Pygmalion.

305. He had a kelpy beard.

306. He made Delphinus a constellation in the sky.

307. Neptune.

308. His wife and children.

309. 1.F, 2.D, 3.A, 4.E, 5.B, 6.C.

310. Ceres.

311. Atlas.

312. A dolphin. The lyre.
313. Polyphemus.
314. Periander.
315. Atalanta.

THE TWELVE TASKS
OF FLAVIA GEMINA

316. Miriam's betrothal feast.
317. Pistor.
318. His name is Hercules and he is painting the labours of Hercules.
319. Ostrich.
320. Monobaz and Mnason.
321. A witch or enchantress.
322. He thinks she has become too strong-willed and independent.
323. Titus, Felix, Pliny, Titus's brother Domitian.
324. 1. Bring back the head of Medusa. That was Perseus's task.
325. Anus.
326. She isn't wearing her wig.
327. 5. Frigidarium (the cold room).
328. Taurus. He has a mole removed, as it spoilt his looks.
329. He diverted the water downhill from a stream .
330. Taurus's scrapings. If you mix a little of a gladiator's scrapings in someone's food, that person will become passionate towards you.
331. Behind the shrine of the crossroads, at dusk.
332. Diomedes.
333. Scuto.
334. She has one breast uncovered.

335. Greed and passion.

336. She cut off her hair and dedicated it to Diana. She vowed never to marry, and to be a virgin for ever.

337. He is not dead but he divorced Cartilia.

338. They burp heartily after the meal.

339. 6. Sledge pulled by reindeer.

340. Cartilia Poplicola.

341. To make people do exactly as he or she wishes.

342. By the roll of the dice.

343. Lupus.

344. Fever.

345. It has snowed the night before, so Ostia is covered in white.

THE NUMBERS QUIZ

346. Twenty.

347. Dozens.

348. CX (44 + 66 = 110).

349. One hundred.

350. Her price, 600 sesterces.

351. One hundred thousand sesterces.

352. Twenty-five thousand sesterces.

353. C (99 + 1 = 100).

354. B) Eighty feet.

355. One hundred and eighty.

356. 1.E, 2.C, 3.A, 4.B, 5.D.

357. L (20 + 30 = 50).

358. Ten years. Ten. Twenty.

359. The fifteenth.

360. Five.

361. 11 a.m. and 5 in the afternoon.

362. Eight.

363. Sixteen.

364. Thirty.

365. DCC (1000 − 300 = 700).

GLORIOUS FOOD

366. Mint tea.

367. Roast chicken, salad and white rolls.

368. Fish.

369. Camel dung.

370. Dates and grapes.

371. Almonds, dried fish and olive oil.

372. To see if they are still alive.

373. Dark bread that tastes of honey.

374. 1.C, 2.G, 3.A, 4.B, 5.E, 6.D, 7.F.

375. Lemon.

376. Pistachio nuts.

377. Saffron.

378. Pine-nuts and honey.

379. Prawns (honey-glazed).

380. Pomegranate juice.

381. 2. Forks.

382. Mushrooms.

383. Oranges (which were not really known until medieval times).

384. A jar of prunes.

385. 4. Chocolate covered ants (no chocolate in Roman times!).

SHIPS AND SEAFARERS

386. Myrtilla, which was the name of Flavia's mother.
387. Triton.
388. It's a slave ship.
389. By sail and oar.
390. Red and white.
391. The Delphina.
392. There are no banks of oars, just steering paddles at the back.
393. Charybdis.
394. She was a sea-nymph and the mother of Achilles.
395. They eat all the fish, especially his anchovies.
396. A bull.
397. Misenum.
398. Alexandria.
399. 7. Cats were useful for killing vermin.
400. 5. Capua is inland.
401. Sextus.
402. Ethiopia.
403. Pine pitch.
404. He is chanting.
405. Eyes.

THE NAME GAME

406. B. Tawny.
407. A. Twin.
408. A. Wolf.
409. C. Nurse.
410. B. Blockhead.

411. A. Freedman.
412. B. Slave-dealer.
413. A. Old woman.
414. C. One-eyed.
415. C. Lucky.
416. A. Goldsmith.
417. C. Wasp.
418. C. Cat.
419. B. Tiger.
420. C. Soothsayer.
421. B. Shield.
422. C. Bull.
423. B. Spotty.
424. A. Dung.
425. A. Dark.
426. B. Oak.
427. C. Onion.
428. B. Seaweed.
429. B. Beautiful.
430. A. Oily.
431. A. Damp.
432. C. Crumbs.
433. C. Rose.
434. C. Myrtle.
435. A. Red-haired.

GENERAL QUIZ

436. Green Fountain Street.
437. They both have asthma.
438. Actors.
439. Shepenwepet.

440. Pinchas and Eliezar.

441. Sponge-diver.

442. C. Chocolates.

443. A diver.

444. 1.D, 2.E, 3.C, 4.A, 5.G, 6.F, 7.B.

445. Ferocious heat, because it rises in the middle of summer.

446. Because he is driving a delivery cart and no wheeled traffic was allowed in Rome during the hours of daylight (except for the Emperor and vestal virgins).

447. The Tomb of Cestius.

448. It is surrounded on three sides by the sea.

449. Because he has heard stories of entire apartment blocks collapsing without notice.

450. Vespasian, who died in June of AD 79.

451. The world.

452. They need to apply the paint to the damp white plaster before it dries.

453. His headaches.

454. The Colosseum.

455. 6. Vestal virgins.

456. Fire and crime.

457. Sing it.

458. People mix the old wine with the new.

459. Jupiter, Juno and Minerva.

460. Phosphorescence.

461. Sorrento.

462. Greek.

463. Gaius Plinius Phrixus.

464. Book Six.

465. Games/races/festival.

466. Water.

467. Imperator = Emperor.

468. Cupid.

469. Unus, duo, tres, quattuor, quinque, sex.

470. Denarius.

471. Equestrians.

472. Yom Kippur, also known as the Day of Atonement.

473. Shalom.

474. A dining room.

475. Beware of the dog.

476. A gladiator school.

477. Augustus.

478. The Emperor Nero.

479. Mithras.

480. Colourful cloth conical hats such as freedmen wore.

481. Flavia's cook and former nursemaid.

482. It's covered with vineyards.

483. Marcus Artorius Bato.

484. Emperor Titus's younger brother.

485. Pumice.

NUBIA-ISMS

486. G. Phosphorescence.

487. D. Mount Olympus.

488. H. Rubric.

489. J. Assassin.

490. E. Nero and Poppaea.

491. F. Loaded dice.

492. A. Pessimist.

493. B. Sponge-diver.

494. I. Immortality.

495. C. Divitiae.

OUTTAKES

ABOUT THE CONTRIBUTORS

Roisin Corbett is eleven years old. Some of you may remember her appearance on *Junior Mastermind* in 2006 where she won her heat with all correct answers. Her special subject was, of course, the Roman Mysteries! Her favourite book is *The Sirens of Surrentum* because of its many twists and turns. Nubia is her favourite character, because she is a flautist (like Roisin herself) and because 'she senses things about people that others don't notice.'

S.R.H. James is a London-based Latin and Games schoolmaster who happens to have visited Sorrento twenty times. Perhaps it's no surprise that his favourite Roman Mysteries book is *The Sirens of Surrentum* (but he also relishes the unflinching violent descriptions of *The Gladiators of Capua*). His favourite character changes weekly, but at the moment it's probably Pulchra or Pollius Felix.

Yusra Qazi is thirteen and lives in Canada. He comments, 'All the books are so great but I like *The Assassins of Rome* the best because Jonathan is my favourite character in the series. There are countless similarities between us.' He is looking forward to finding out more about Jonathan in future books.

Pekka Tuomisto is a Latin scholar who lives in Finland, where she works as a researcher, translator and nonfiction writer. Of all the Roman Mysteries, she especially likes *The Pirates of Pompeii*, because it takes the reader deep into the real-life events – and shows that, despite everything, life always goes on. Her favourite character is Lupus, whom she says 'needs much cunning and courage to cope with other people – and has both in ample measure!'

Rowan Ellis Williams-Fletcher is fifteen years old. Her favourite character is Cartilia from *The Twelve Tasks of Flavia Gemina* because of the many misconceptions about her, the role she plays in Flavia's life at the time and the dramatic storyline surrounding her. Her favourite book in the series is *The Dolphins of Laurentum*, because not only has it got the good old traditional treasure hunt but it's also the book where Lupus's past is *finally* revealed – which makes for a cliff-hanging read.

Emma Yeomans is ten years old. In 2005, when she was eight, she won the *Times*/Short Books Great Young Historians competition (for the under tens) with a letter written to Admiral Pliny (inspired, of course, by the Roman Mysteries). Of her entry, Simon Schama said, 'I somehow think Pliny Sr. would have loved this and have written back – in several volumes.' Emma's favourite character is Nubia because she is kind and understanding. Her favourite Roman Mystery is *The Fugitive From Corinth*.

And about the series' author, Caroline Lawrence . . .

Caroline Lawrence is a Californian who came to England to study Classics and has now lived in the UK longer than she lived in the US. Her favourite Roman Mystery is *The Pirates of Pompeii*, because she enjoyed writing it so much that at times 'had to be physically dragged away from the keyboard'. Her favourite character is Flavia Gemina, because 'Flavia is a bossy know-it-all like me, but also a truth-seeker.'

THE SECOND
ROMAN MYSTERIES
QUIZ BOOK

Are you ready to test your knowledge of yet more brilliant Roman Mysteries novels? As well as questions on the events and characters in books 7-12 of the series, there are quizzes about Roman Entertainment, Rules and Rituals, Architecture, Medicine, Love and Marriage. Plus ... there are more picture puzzles to solve and another mammoth general quiz about life in ancient Rome.

TRIMALCHO'S FEAST
AND OTHER MINI-MYSTERIES

Between writing her bestselling novels, Caroline Lawrence has penned several short stories, covering incidents alluded to in the novels, but not dramatised at length. This book brings together all the mini-mysteries to provide complete coverage of events in the lives of our four detectives. Each of these short and sharp stories is as compelling and exciting as the novels, full of the sights and sounds of ancient Rome.

To find out more about Caroline Lawrence
and the Roman Mysteries visit

www.romanmysteries.com